For Annie, whose compassion and support are limitless.
–S.C.

To Wayne, for always helping.
–E.U.

An imprint of Rodale Books
733 Third Avenue, New York, NY 10017
Visit us online at RodaleKids.com.

Rodale Kids books may be purchased for business or promotional use
or for special sales. For information, please e-mail: RodaleKids@Rodale.com.

Printed in China
Manufactured by RRD Asia 201804

Design by Jeff Shake
Text set in Report School
The artwork for this book was created with pencil and paper,
then painted digitally in Adobe Photoshop.

Library of Congress Cataloging-in-Publication Data is on file with the publisher.

ISBN 978-1-62336-960-6 paperback
ISBN 978-1-62336-962-0 hardcover

Distributed to the trade by Macmillan
10 9 8 7 6 5 4 3 2 1 paperback
10 9 8 7 6 5 4 3 2 1 hardcover

It is going to be
a great day.

Mom and Dad are bringing
my new baby sister
home today.
I can't wait!

I help Grandma get
the twins up.
All dressed.

Breakfast served.

Teeth brushed.

Ready for baby!
Grandma tells me
that I am helpful.

At last, they are home.
Baby Emily looks bigger
and cuter than she did
in the hospital!
Mom looks tired.
She looks so happy, too.

I know what to do.
I help Dad unpack.

While Mom rests, Grandma shows me how to hold Emily. Sometimes we give Emily a bottle.

I even help change
her diaper.
Pee-yew!

The days fly by.
Soon Grandma goes
home to Grandpa.
It's up to me to be
Mom and Dad's helper.
I've got this.

Sometimes it is
all about Emily.

Sometimes it is
all about the twins.
They can make
a lot of noise.

And then Emily
makes a lot of noise!
I know what to do.

We can go outside
to play.

Or we can stay inside
and read.
I am helpful.

Sometimes I want
it to be all about me.
Math can be tricky.
And Mom is really
good at it.

But Emily is teething.
So Mom has
her hands full.

Dad is busy, too.
He is putting
the twins to bed.

I figure it out.
Helping myself
is another way
to be helpful.

We take a trip to visit
Grandma and Grandpa.
It is Grandpa's birthday.

Emily is excited.

She is crawling
everywhere.

Finally, it is
party time.
I help in the kitchen.

Then I set the table.

23

Now it is
time to eat!

I put Emily
in her high chair.
Then I set up her food.

There is so much
good food to eat!
Everyone is talking
and laughing.

Emily wants to join in.
She has something to say.
She blurts out a word.

It is her first word.
Everyone stops eating.
We look at Emily.
Emily looks at us.

She points to me
and says "June!"
She said my name!

I love my family.
It feels good
to help when I can.
I am helpful.

When do
YOU
feel helpful?

Can you think of
three examples?

Also available:

I Am Smart

Look for these other titles in the
POSITIVE POWER series:

- **I Am Thankful**
- **I Am Kind**
- **I Am Brave**
- **I Am Strong**

To learn more about Rodale Kids Curious Readers,
please visit RodaleKids.com.

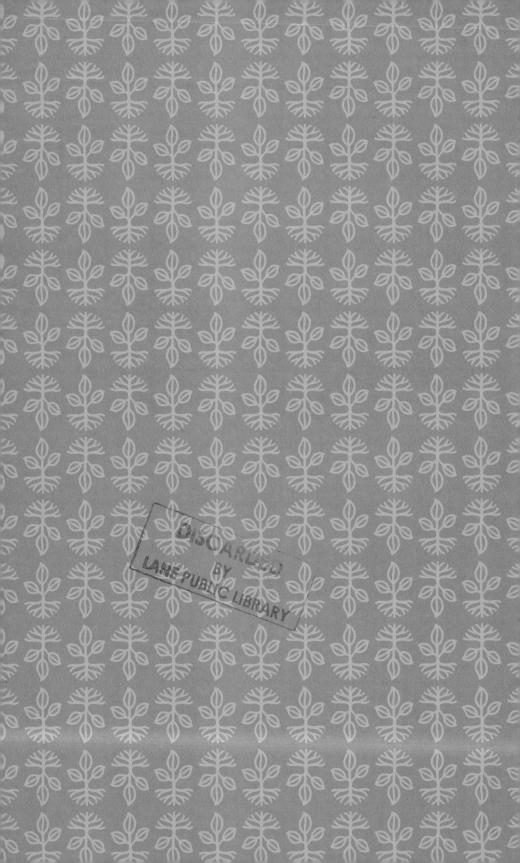